Milo's Toothache

Milo's Toothache

by Ida Luttrell
pictures by Enzo Giannini

Dial Books for Young Readers · New York

Published by
Dial Books for Young Readers
A Division of Penguin Books USA Inc.
375 Hudson Street
New York, New York 10014

Printed in Hong Kong by
South China Printing Company (1988) Limited

The Dial Easy-to-Read logo is a registered trademark of
Dial Books for Young Readers,
a division of Penguin Books USA Inc., ® TM 1,162,718.

Library of Congress Cataloging in Publication Data
Luttrell, Ida.
Milo's toothache/by Ida Luttrell; pictures by Enzo Giannini.
p.   cm.
Summary: Milo Pig plans to visit the dentist about his toothache,
but his friends overreact and make the outing into a big problem.
ISBN 0-8037-1034-8 (trade). –ISBN 0-8037-1035-6 (lib.)
[1. Dental care — Fiction. 2. Pigs — Fiction.] I. Giannini, Enzo,
ill. II. Title.   PZ7.L97953Mi 1992   [E] — dc20   91-24315   CIP   AC

First Edition
1 3 5 7 9 10 8 6 4 2

The full-color artwork was prepared using pencil, colored pencils,
and watercolors. It was then scanner-separated and reproduced
as red, blue, yellow, and black halftones.

Reading Level 2.0

To my friend, Susan Cohen,
with much appreciation
–I.L.

To my dentist, Dr. Barsh
–E.G.

Milo Pig and his friend Dan
were playing Ping-Pong
in Milo's kitchen.

"Ouch!" Milo said. "My tooth hurts."

"Oh, no," said Dan,

"now you will have to go to a dentist!"

"That is a good idea," said Milo,

and he went to the phone.

When Milo hung up, he told Dan,

"The dentist can see me today

at four o'clock."

"Today!" Dan cried. "We need to hurry
and put this stuff away
so I can go home to change."
Dan rushed to pick up the balls.

"Why should *you* hurry?" Milo asked.
"I am the one with the toothache."

"Because I am going too," said Dan,

"so you won't be afraid."

"I am not afraid," said Milo.

"You will be when you get there,"

Dan said on his way to the door.

"Don't be silly," said Milo.

"The dentist will make

my tooth stop hurting."

"You will be glad I am there," said Dan.

"Come if you want to," Milo said.

"But now I am going to take a bath."

Dan headed home.

Oh, my gosh! he thought.

What if *I* get scared?

I will get Amy to come with me.

Dan ran to Amy's house.

"Amy, Amy," he yelled.

"Milo is in terrible pain.

He has to go to the dentist!

We had better go with him

so that he won't be afraid.

Can you come?"

"Sure," said Amy.

Dan raced home to get ready.

The clock ticked on

at Milo's house.

Milo relaxed in his nice warm bath.

16

Amy went to the mirror
to see if she looked brave.
"Oh, dear," she said.
"If Dan gets scared,
then *I* will be scared."

Amy ran out of her house in a panic.
She found her friend Pam playing ball
with Art and Ira, the twins next door.
"Pam," cried Amy, "it's an emergency!
Dan and I are rushing Milo
to the dentist.
I am helping Dan help Milo be brave.
Can you come?"

"Of course," said Pam,

and she threw the ball on the porch.

"We will come too," said Art and Ira.

Milo's clock showed
it was time to go.
So Milo got out of the tub
and put on his clothes.

Amy, Pam, Ira, and Art ran
to Dan's house.
Amy banged on the door.

Dan opened it and said,
"Thank goodness you are here!
Milo must be a wreck by now."

They rushed down the street together
in a loud bumping crowd.

Milo heard them coming.

"What is going on?" he asked.

Dan was out of breath.

"We are coming with you," he said,

"so you won't be afraid."

"I give up," said Milo. "Let's go."

They walked quickly to the corner.

Art pointed and cried,

"There is the dentist's office!

Are you scared yet, Milo?"

"No," Milo said.

"Why should I be scared?"

They all began to talk at once.

Ira ran to keep up with them.

"My aunt had a sore tooth once,"
he said. "The dentist pulled it
and she had to eat mush for a week."
"Oh!" said Dan, grabbing his jaw.
"That's awful! My uncle went
to the dentist and..."

"What happened?" Pam asked.

"I don't want to hear it!" Milo shouted,
and covered his ears.

"See," Dan said,

"Milo is getting scared.

It is a good thing we came with him,"

he added as they stepped up to

the dentist's office.

Milo opened the door

to the waiting room.

All his friends crowded in.

They sat down.

There was no seat left for Milo.

So he sat on the floor.

The office door creaked.

Milo's friends all jumped up

and yelled, "THE DENTIST!"

"Be quiet," said Milo. "I won't hear
my name when she calls me."

The dentist looked

into the waiting room.

"Milo, you are next," she said.

Milo followed the dentist
and the door closed behind him.
Dan, Amy, Pam, and the twins
sat on the edge of their chairs
and waited.
They heard the dentist say,
"Open wide, Milo."

Dan fainted.

Art and Ira jumped up to help him.

They bumped heads.

Ira fell on Amy's foot.

Amy grabbed her foot

and hopped up from her chair.

Her elbow jabbed Pam's nose.

Pam yelled.

The door opened and Milo was back.

He heard, "OUCH, OOCH, OW!"

He saw Dan on the floor,

Art's black eye, Ira's fat lip,

Amy hopping up and down,

and Pam's nose as big as a potato.

"Now I know why you were afraid
to come here," said Milo.

Dan sat up.

"Because it hurt?" he asked.

"No!" Milo said. "It was only popcorn between my teeth. I am fine! But you all need to go to a doctor."

"A *doctor*!" they yelled.

"Don't worry," said Milo.

"I will go with you."